MW00583561

Robert Scheffer (1863-1926) was born the son of a clergyman at Colmar Alsace. He became private secretary to Carmen Sylva Queen of Romania and later, in 1891, went to Paris to devote himself to literature, becoming a contributed to many of the leading magazines, including the *Mercure de France* and the *Revue blanche*. He produced numerous volumes of prose and verse, including *Misère royale* (1893), *Hermeros* (1899), and *Les Frissonnantes* (1905).

robert scheffer

THE GREEN FLY
AND OTHER STORIES

THIS IS A SNUGGLY BOOK

Copyright © 2023 by Snuggly Books
All rights reserved.

ISBN: 978-1-64525-137-8

CONTENTS

THE GREEN FLY
AND OTHER STORIES

THE GREEN FLY

IT is done now, and the future will show whether I was wrong to marry again. But my solitude had really become intolerable, and my health demanded that I take into my life a companion whose presence and caresses will, I hope, drive away my nightmares. While there are fine solitudes that are made beautiful by dreams and mystery, mine, on the contrary, is peopled with terrible visions. I am persecuted by invisible beings that sometimes manifest themselves to my eyes under the strangest and most cruel forms. There was fault on my side, I know, and by committing the crime I raised against myself the powers of hell. But it has lasted too long, and the soothing influence of Claire, my new wife, should disarm the other, the first one, who pursues me incessantly, in darkness and in light, seeking to avenge herself.

I gaze upon Claire as she sleeps. She does not suspect that my anguish is soothed by the sight of her peaceful slumber and that she is the charming fairy who will drive away the ill-omened crew of phantoms that float along the tapestried walls in the ancient and somber nuptial chamber and swarm down on me from above the vaulted windows, twining in and out among the velvet shadows of the heavy curtains. She is pretty and frail under the cambric cover that, chastely slipping from her shoulders, reveals the rounded contour of her bosom; nestling among the laces of the pillow, her golden hair flowing over her face and her eyes closed, she smiles in her sleep.

For a long time I gazed at her. The purity of her dreams has crept into my accursed soul and softly shines there. But—I know not what terror has suddenly contracted my heart! It seemed to me that, under my persistent gaze, her features changed, modeling themselves on those of the other, of Madeleine, who is dead. Her expression altered simultaneously, her breathing became labored, she moved, sighed, her eyelids fluttered and, when she awoke, I read terror in her eyes as I leaned over her to reassure her. Just such awakenings had I secretly observed before in Madeleine in the old days.

"Is it day yet?" she asked. "You are already up? I've had a horrid dream—I do not know quite what——" I took her in my arms and caressed her, and presently she fell asleep again like a child, with one arm lying above her head.

But I was not mistaken, and I wonder that I had not noticed it earlier, that she recalls Madeleine, though I cannot say precisely in what features, for her heavy hair was black with steely blue lights in it.

Madeleine—my thoughts are completely filled with her and with that night when I thought the sinister past was buried. I certainly had the right to kill her inasmuch as she had betrayed me, and so it is not remorse for the act itself that pursues me, but for the manner in which I took my revenge.

From a long line of ancestors I inherited a crafty and vindictive nature. Frankness has no place in my mental processes, though I decide unerringly on the end to be attained. Dissimulation is to me a habitual garment, and I have no need to lie, so completely have I accustomed myself not to uncover the truth that I wish to stifle or the suspicion that should not be aroused. My forte lies in knowing what not to say. And so when I suspected Madeleine of being unfaithful to me I took pains not to betray my jealousy to her. On the contrary, I acted frankly and cordially toward her and afforded her easy opportunities to sin, in such wise that I had abundant liberty to assure myself that my suspicions were well founded.

And then, though my blood fairly boiled, I did not break out, I did not have recourse to the dagger or the foolish bullet. More than ever I schooled my face and my manner, and from what I know she suspected nothing. I fairly exhaled confidence, and Madeleine felt herself perfectly safe. However, she complained of vague ills, and her health, which until then had been superb, began to fail. She could not tell precisely what ailed her; as for me, I reassured her and lavished the tenderest care on her. As she drooped from day to day (I gave the poison in very minute doses) she was soon unable to leave her room, and then even her bed. If I had killed her brutally I would have deprived myself of the pleasure of watching the secret anguish that consumed her, and therein lies the superiority of a patient over a swift vengeance. For in her isolation, of which I was the jailer, Madeleine received no message from her lover, nor could she have him brought to her. I read in her eyes her mute and incessant despair; I understood her mental torture, far worse than her physical suffering, and, lavishing hypocritical cares upon her, I reveled in her hatred toward me that she dared not express.

That lasted a week, two weeks; then, at the time I had fixed, her death agony began. Madeleine became delirious, and standing at her bedside I savagely repeated after her the

confessions of her delirium. A little while before she died she had a lucid interval. I took
her in my arms as if to give her a final kiss,
and whispered, "It is I who have killed you,"
and clearly, emphasizing it with all my anger,
all my accumulated scorn, I hissed an epithet
in her ear. Her eyes grew wide, a terrible light
flamed up in them. She made a threatening
gesture, mumbled a few incomprehensible
syllables; then a spasm seized her, and her head
fell back motionless in the funereal waves of
her black hair.

Since she was dead, I wept, and the people
who were present pitied my great sorrow. I
watched beside her through two nights, recall-
ing in the presence of her remains the tender
joys of former days and the bitter ecstasies of
the past fortnight; and I know not what strange
fear, against which I could not defend myself,
crept over me as I gazed upon my victim, who
seemed to live once more in the flickering light
of the tapers. Dawn was whitening the heavens;
the windows were filled with its pallid light;
the strangeness of the hour augmented my

anxiety; worn out with fatigue, I was almost fainting and wished fervently that the funeral ceremonies might be quickly ended.

Suddenly in the silence sounded the droning of a rapid, whirling flight; something vibrated near me, lighting up the shadows with a fitful glitter. All at once a hideous fly alighted on the lips of the dead. Its green corselet glistened under its diaphanous wings; from its head, of a metallic green, darted a tongue, and tranquilly it absorbed the ichor of the dead body.

The spectacle filled me with disgust. I raised my hand. The fly rose in slow flight, disappeared behind the curtains, and I heard its buzzing fade away into the distance, then grow nearer again. Suddenly it struck me on the mouth, it clung there! The sensation was revolting! It seemed to me that I had been sullied by this con tact with the dead, by an unclean kiss. I uttered a cry; everything swam before my eyes, and I fainted. No one has ever known that, at the instant when I sank into the black abyss, I understood that the soul of the dead had taken possession of my flesh.

Since then, and often, I have seen Madeleine's face, intangible and implacable; I have felt the weight of her arms pressing on my throat as if to strangle me; the cold wind of her breath has frozen my face; and time and again the green fly has come back, imprisoning me in the circle of its glittering flight, lightly touching my hair, my eyelids and violating my mouth, on which it surely and promptly alights. Many times have I tried to crush it. It easily evaded me and in triumph made me dizzy with its rapid flight and its droning. Its presence has become a torment to me. In spite of lights the horrible nights have inflicted it on me, and when dawn came, sleep fleeing my eyes, it has been still worse.

But the round of evil phantoms was swept away under the sovereign influence of a young and innocent creature, and already, like the incense that spreads through a chapel, Claire's breath has purified the atmosphere, in which peace reigns once more.

Look—behind the raised curtains it is not the pallid dawn, it is the sunrise that is already reddening the windows, and soon the first golden arrows of the sun will implant in me the joy of living and of loving Claire, whose morning kiss announces to me my resurrection.

But what is this? An emerald spark has plowed through the space where the light is diffused, a familiar buzzing assails my ears, and—ah, I have crushed it on my lips—the fly, the horrible green fly!

A month has passed. My prediction was right. I have regained my former serenity, and from this time forth it is unalterable, for a barrier of ingenuousness has been raised between me and the terrible beyond, a barrier impassable by adverse powers. Claire is a delightful companion, whose grace will make my dark years beautiful; she is a child who will make me young again, and there is no care that does not give way before the gentle pressure of her cool hand on my forehead. Springtime lives in her limpid eyes. From her emanates a revivifying perfume, and to make me bend to her light caprices she talks like the little girl she is and does with me whatever she will.

Still, one thing in her troubles me. She speaks too often of Madeleine. She imagines that I love that first wife passionately, that I will always prefer her. She questions me about her tastes, her manners, her toilets. She wishes to resemble her, in order to combine in her own person both the present and the past, so that she alone shall be mistress of all my thoughts. And sometimes her face seems to me—under what breath?—to tremble like a wave under the breeze, the golden glory of her hair is dimmed, her expression is changed, her face—yes, it is true!—her face is altered and her eyes regard me with what threatening irony!

"Madeleine, Madeleine!" I cry, and then, delighted, she kisses me and says:

"Oh, you naughty man, not to be satisfied with your little Claire and wanting her to lead our beloved to you by the hand I am doing my best; every day I am making progress."

But her caresses calm me; the interposed image is effaced, and, pressing her to me, I murmur:

"No, you are Claire, my darling, my golden-haired fairy, and it is you alone that I love."

But she shakes her head mutinously and replies: "That is not true."

My peace was of short duration, and evil powers make sport of my most subtle calculations.

This morning Claire entered my workroom, as was her custom. Scarcely. was she on the threshold, where she paused an instant in smiling hesitation, when her fair presence seemed to diffuse a brightness throughout the great, gloomy room, in which the light coming through the Gothic windows threw strange shadows on the floor. Like a sylph suddenly stopped in her flight, she waited until I should call her before springing toward me. That morning I had a sudden feeling, from the very moment that she stopped at the threshold, that it was not she, but the other, who was entering the room. A violet shadow tarnished the gold of her hair; her movements were constrained; her face was changed, and she wore an old gown of Madeleine's that she had made over. She held herself erect before me, her hands joined on her breast, in the stiff attitude of a portrait.

"We have left Claire in the dressingroom," she said, "and it is Madeleine who has come to pay you a visit."

Even the quality of her voice was changed.

The fancy displeased me. I contracted my brows and was preparing a reprimand, when all at once my sight became blurred.

"Oh!" I cried. "Drive it away, destroy it; I cannot bear to look at it!"

On her corsage crawled the fly, the green fly, glittering and malevolent.

"Why, what's the matter?" asked Claire, making a little face. "What am I to drive away?"

Her cautious fingers glided over the soft silk, on which the fly still remained.

"The fly, the devilish green fly!" I cried, not daring to approach her.

She burst out in merry laughter. "Were you taken in by that? It is only a brooch, and a beautiful piece of workmanship. See," and she detached the jewel, which was composed of emeralds and diamonds in exact reproduction of a fly with diaphanous wings, and held it before my eyes.

Instinctively I drew back, and by I know not what chance the point of the pin scratched my lip, on which a drop of blood welled up at once. The contact made me shudder; the old horror had laid hold of me again, and with a violent movement I flung the jewel to the floor.

"Oh, have I hurt you?" cried Claire. "How awkward I am! Forgive me!"

And kneeling before me she patted the scratch with her handkerchief. I felt that I was ridiculous, but I could not master my emotion.

"It is nothing," I managed to say at last. "But—I do not recognize this jewel. Where did you get it?"

"You do not recognize it?" She smiled with an air of mystery. "Why, I thought I would please you by putting it on. It was shut up in a little case which had evidently been overlooked in the drawer of a secretary that belonged to Madeleine."

"Ah," was all I said, but a horrible pain seized me. I was certain that I had never seen that brooch on Madeleine's neck. I knew that it must have come to her from her lover and that she had not dared to wear it in my presence.

I picked up the green fly, which lay where it had fallen on the floor, stepped quickly to the open window, and threw it far out.

"Ah, that is better," I said, greatly relieved.

Claire, astonished, said not a word.

That insignificant scratch has festered. I know not what germ of corruption was introduced into my blood through the infected point of the pin. At first I let the thing go; a small abscess formed, but I paid little attention to it. Then I was taken with the violent shivers of a fever.

The doctor who was called in looked very grave.

More and more violent shiverings. I am thirsty. My teeth chatter with unreasoning terror. I think that I am often delirious. In the next chamber I have heard—for my hearing has become singularly acute—these words murmured: "Purulent infection."

I know that I am going to die. Just now Madeleine appeared at the side of my bed. Her lips were set in a horrid grin of triumph.

"In order that vengeance shall be as great as yours," she murmured, "you had to die by the innocent hand of Claire."

I dragged myself up in my bed to curse her. The effort was so great that I lost consciousness. When I came to myself again Claire was stroking my forehead with her cool hand and weeping.

An emerald circle revolves before my eyes, there is a droning, a continual buzzing in my ears that irritates me, terrifies me, which I recognize—Silence—Ah, there it is on the edge of the coverlet, motionless, the fetid green fly, ready to gorge itself on my blood. It is waiting its chance; it is going to throw itself on me. Drive it away! Drive away death! Ah——

THE ROAD OF LONG AGO

I never knew the little town from which my father came. He had sought a fortune and found a wife in a foreign country, where I was born and spent my childhood. But he talked about his birthplace so often that I could see it in the minutest detail, and it seemed to me as if I always had lived there. He expressed frequently, and with an indescribable tenderness, his desire to go back there some day.

What he said annoyed my mother, and I somehow divined that he wanted to make a pious or sentimental pilgrimage of some sort. Death carried him away before he could realize his dream.

Many years later I decided to visit the place, to which a subtle association attached me. The accident of a business trip brought me into the neighborhood. I made a little detour in order to get there.

The image which I had formed corresponded exactly to the reality, except that everything appeared to me tinier than my boyish mind had represented it to be. There was the little square, bordered by houses with sharp and jagged roofs; there was the fountain in the middle of it from which the greenish center basins received a parsimonious flow of water; there were the streets, narrowed by arcades which sheltered the darkened shops; there was the massive church alongside the canal and the group of linden trees, under which the town notables chatted. An old lady passed by, fragile and stooping, one might have said, under the weight of her big hat. I was prompted to greet her as a venerable friend.

I spent some time gazing at my father's home, which I recognized without difficulty. I should have liked to go through it, but feared that a request for permission to do so might excite ridicule. So I contented myself with contemplating the delicate facade, with its curious sixteenth-century carvings, and the corner tower, from which my father used to watch the infrequent passers-by. Then, leaving the town, I wandered into the country.

The horizon was suddenly enlarged. Some mountains stretched away in a long curve above the broad plain, which sizzled under the powerful summer sun. In contrast with this immensity the town itself looked smaller than ever, sharp in its contours and with a curious relief, heightened by its reddish tint. The road which I followed wound through wheat fields and then through vineyards. It next crossed a bare piece of prairie, in which only some walnut trees grew. Further off a line of poplars signaled the presence of the river toward which I was walking and only partially hid a square, white building, whose windows flashed back the sunlight.

A singular thing happened to me. The further I advanced the more I had the feeling of no longer being myself. Another being was substituted for my own. It was my father's soul, which had entered into me. I saw myself walking along as if in a mirror. In the same way I lost all sense of time and was carried back to a distant period in which I was making the same journey. I? No, not I, but my father. This mental state, however vague and disconcerting, didn't surprise me, and it was accompanied with unusually pleasurable thoughts.

How delightful the day was, with its generous warmth, and what sweet odors arose from the prairie exhaled by flowers which, though humble, seemed imbued with passionate life! I plucked some flowers and made a rustic bouquet, which recalled I know not what memory of the past.

I crossed the river and found myself facing the white house. Before it was a gilded iron gate, opening on a lawn. This lawn was ornamented with a fountain, encircled by trees. All the windows of the house were shut and it seemed uninhabited. I entered the gate as if that was the most natural thing in the world for me to do.

The lodgekeeper came out of his lodge and asked me if I wished to visit the park. He told me that in the absence of the owner the place was opened to citizens who cared to enjoy its shade. Noticing my bouquet, he smiled:

"You will find much rarer flowers here," he said. "And if you love flowers———"

But I shook my head. The flowers I had sufficed me.

I was free to wander alone up and down the silent walks.

"There were fetes here," I thought, "and then they suddenly stopped."

I repeated this reflection, searching in my mind for a recollection which eluded me. I walked ahead, however, as in the halo of a dream, toward some undefined goal. My mind vibrated to fugitive impressions—to reminiscences which I couldn't pin down.

I seated myself for a moment on a bench in the shade of a chestnut tree. I listened to the warblings of the birds. A leaf fell on my knees.

At that light shock, tumultuous sensations were awakened within me. A vision took form, disappeared and then reappeared—that of a young girl who was looking at me. It seemed as if a hand was placed on my shoulder and a voice murmured: "Go further."

I arose. I saw no one. Nevertheless, I felt no astonishment that someone had been seated there at my side—just now or years ago? It made little difference when, for I no longer had any sense of time. But I was sure that there was a presence near me, and that we two would accompany each other wherever I went.

Turning this way and that way I reached the end of the park, where a lonely group of cypresses stood guard about some gravestones. There was nothing mournful about this little cemetery. It presented itself, rather, as a refuge where peace reigned. I bent down over the graves to read the names. I was especially struck by this inscription:

"Marie d'Yrecourt, 1862-1882."

My eyes moistened, my heart softened and, with a pious gesture, as if I were accomplishing a long delayed rite, I laid on the stone the flowers which I had gathered along the roadside.

At that moment it seemed to me as if a fog had lifted, as if I had returned to myself and, with changed eyes, was gazing at the things about me. Why had I come to this place? Why had I laid my flowers on that grave? I read the inscription again: "Marie d'Yrecourt." I had heard that name spoken by my father, always mysteriously and tenderly. That was the date—1882—when he left his native city, never to return to it.

Meditating for a long time, evoked the romance of his life, his betrothal, the young girl's death, his incurable regret, his persistent desire to go back and to kneel before this gravestone. And I understood that he himself had conducted me there, with the flowers.

So, with a full knowledge of what I was doing, it was I who knelt.

THE MOTHER

HOW and when Jacques and I became friends matters very little. I think he takes pleasure in my society because it is natural to me to speak my mind without reticence or reserve.—In this way we are human complements. On the outbreak of war we lost sight of each other; all I knew of him was that his thorough knowledge of German had enabled him to offer his services as an interpreter. Towards the end of last year we met again, and his work keeping him since that time in Paris, we renewed, so far as his duties permitted, our old companionship. There was little change in either of us, and the accounts he gave of his experiences were immensely interesting to one who had vegetated while so much was doing, and could contribute nothing to the war but idle speculations. I remarked, however, the imprint of suffering in the lines of his face, which I thought was not to be wondered at considering the nature of his work. But it appeared there was a more intimate and secret cause for it.

Yesterday afternoon he came to me in a nervous, agitated state, altogether unlike himself. Before I could ask any questions, he broke out, pacing the floor with long strides:

"I must speak. I must tell my trouble to someone. It has been making me miserable all through the war, and today I feel as if my heart is breaking."

I was completely taken aback. He saw it, and went on more calmly:

"Oh! I've not committed any crime. It's sorrow, and sorrow of a most intimate kind. Let me tell you about it; perhaps that will ease my mind. You know nothing, or next to nothing, of my family, except that my father was a worthy man, a wine-merchant, and that he left me my small income. But my mother—well, though her name was French, my mother was a German.

"My mother had never been able to adapt herself to French ways and manners, and at Paris hankered incessantly after the Baden district where she was born. How the marriage came about I do not exactly know; it was a case of love on my father's side, I believe, but more especially one of mutual interests affecting the two families.

"I was an only child, and my parents were devoted to me. My father, who considered me gifted beyond my years, imagined a brilliant career for me; I was to study law, was to be a barrister, Member of Parliament, a Minister. My mother shook her head; she would have liked me to be a poet, a musician, and though she did not put it into words, she believed that I should find Germany the country most suited to my talents and character.

"How can I describe my mother. Dreamy and sentimental, she passed part of every day at the piano, absorbed in Mendelssohn or Schumann; she loved to interpret Wagner to me, and growing exalted as she played, a dreamy mysticism used to fill her eyes as she said: 'Listen intently: it is the soul of my country overflowing and shedding its blessing on you.' I loved that music, and as I listened, my mother's charming face, beautified by her exaltation, symbolized for me the country of her birth. I did not care so much for the poetry she used to read me—Uhland, Geibel, or Schiller, whom she considered incomparable. I did not understand them; and when she tried to make me like the patriotic poems of Arndt or Koerner, my whole soul rebelled. Some instinctive revolt made me remember that my father was French, and I told her so. Then she would stroke my hair and say sadly: 'Poor child, you ought to have had a different father.'

"My father knew nothing of all this; he fully believed that in spite of her German ways, his wife was quite content with her adopted country, and he never troubled himself about my double heredity and its possible influence.

And no harm might have come from it had he lived, but he died before I had grown out of boyhood, and the course of my existence was entirely changed.

"My mother went back to live with her family, and under the pretext that it would be useful for me to know German thoroughly, I was sent to a boarding-school at Heilbronn, Württemberg. I was not happy there—not that they ill-treated me, but they were completely tactless, making me feel their, not hostility towards the French, but a kind of sympathetic pity. For example, one day when a professor had been extolling the virtues and greatness of Germany, he said to me: 'You have a share in all this. You are half-German, and the day will come when you will have to be wholly German.' And he went on to describe the dream of Germany ruling the world and regenerating mankind under the inspiring genius of the Emperor. I protested hotly; but he only burst into a fit of laughter in which my schoolfellows joined.

"I spent my holidays alternately with relatives of my father or with my mother. My mother . . . I hardly recognized her, she had so completely changed. She had bloomed into a different kind of being. Dreamy and wistful in bygone days, she was now expansive and full of merriment. She laughed heartily at the broadest German jokes. The keyboard of the piano was no longer touched with dreamy restraint; its notes thundered. Her voice vibrated as she sang passionate 'lieder.' She dressed richly and with a bad taste that shocked me. She had become an excessive eater. I could not bear to see her enjoying an atmosphere of pretentious vulgarity. She would kiss me, saying: 'Well, you're happy here, Jacques, aren't you? You feel that you're lucky to be growing up among a race of wonderful people, don't you?' And she would run on interminably in the same strain, repeating that she was happy, and taking no notice of my uneasiness. Her brother—my uncle—noticed it for her. 'Oh, the little Frenchie!' he scoffed, 'he is prejudiced against us now, but the day will come when he will have to love us!' I thought of my father and all he had told me of the agonies of 1870, and my eyes filled with tears.

"Happy, yes, my mother was happy, more than happy, and in a way I little imagined. One evening—it was during the Easter holidays—she beckoned me to her side. An air of great festivity permeated the house, which I put down to preparations for Easter. But I was wrong. Without any leading up to it, she said: 'Jacques, I am going to be married.' I stared at her, stupefied. She laughed. 'You think I'm too old for that?' No, my mother was still quite young, younger than I had ever known her, exuberant to an overwhelming degree. My throat contracted with a kind of anguish.

"'And who is it?' I murmured.

"'Dr. Weber.'

"Dr. Weber, red-faced, fat, gold-spectacled, vain, prosy . . .

"'A German,' I cried.

"'Naturally,' she replied.

"A heart-twist sent burning tears to my eyes . . . She looked at me with cold displeasure, reproaching me for being too sensitive and shutting my eyes to the realities of life. But later on she kissed me, assuring me that the marriage would make no change in our relationship; then she praised the attainments and character of my future stepfather, and finally I was dismissed with the information that she had made all arrangements for completing my education, and that I was free to choose my path in life—in Germany or in France.

"I could not bear the idea of meeting Dr. Weber again, and next day I took refuge with some relations of my father.

"For a long time I reproached myself bitterly for having acted like this towards my mother. It was about 1895, and there was at that period no hatred of Germany, rather an instinctive antipathy not unmingled with admiration. But it was no use reasoning with myself; I felt a kind of shame about this second marriage; it seemed to me that in some subtle way the humiliation involved me, and that sensation was strong enough to make me recoil from companionship in directions where my parentage was known.

"From that time onwards I knew nothing of my mother but what her letters told me. Yet I loved her, and loved her with all the more ardor because I needed her and she was so far away. I read her letters eagerly, trying to discover in them some token of affection and tenderness. If there had been one word of real love, I would have asked forgiveness, and would have approached her husband in a friendly spirit. But they were frigid, with a forbidding note of pedantry in their eternal good advice, and when she told me she had given birth to a son, Eric, I knew the separation was definite, and that for her I had become a foreigner.

"Study and travel in different countries kept me from dwelling on my curious orphanhood, and I grew to look on it with a calmness that verged on indifference. Or I thought I did. But indifference is apparently only a passing sleep of the feelings, for I have just had an experience that has awakened emotions which prove that, though I have not heard from her since the outbreak of war, nothing can alter my love for her.

"You know that a few days ago a Zeppelin was brought down near Paris. The pilot, dangerously wounded, was taken prisoner. I have not seen him, but his papers were sent to me for translation. There were letters addressed to 'Lieutenant Eric Weber' and—they were in my mother's, handwriting!

"I cannot describe the agony with which I read those letters, the misery of having to translate them for others. And my suffering was not caused by the fact that my brother, my half-brother, had come over to try to murder our civilians; it was as the son of my mother that I suffered. For all the letters began 'My only son; My dear and only son . . .' Apparently I have ceased to exist for her.

"Has she forgotten me? Has she abjured me? My mother is alive, and yet I have no mother. Can you realize what that means, you who have a mother, a real French mother, who loves you dearly?"

DORA NANI

PALE and careworn, in a costume of deep mourning, and with prayer-book in hand, Madame Dolland, widow, was following out a daily custom by directing her footsteps toward her favorite chapel, when at the corner of the street a conspicuous placard attracted her attention.

In the town of Z——, the largest of the district and a city of the third class, distractions were rare and everything an event. Even the walls were stupid, and a colored poster which by chance enlivened their dullness was an object of comment; so that Madame Dolland, widow, drew near to examine it.

She gave a start and grew dizzy; the prayer book slipped from her trembling hands. With difficulty she recovered it and, gaining her composure, took courage to look again. Yes, she had read it aright—Dora Nani.

It was she; Dora Nani, the well-known tragedienne, this conspicuous woman with neck and shoulders bare and covered with jewels; with figure immodestly draped in flaring red. Yes, it was her likeness which was depicted on the poster.

"The wretched, wretched creature," muttered Madame Dolland, as she finally turned away and, instead of continuing in the direction of the chapel, went back to her own home in tears.

Her only son had killed himself on account of this actress, and here in the small town where his mother had secluded herself they were going to applaud the very woman who had broken her heart.

Why, at that moment when she was absorbed in pious thoughts, was she forced to raise her eyes to the fatal poster! Otherwise she

would not have known and would have continued along in her sad, lonely and resigned
mode of existence, praying for the salvation of
him who had taken his own life; while now—
the past was being revived with its agonies, its
revolts and its despair, and the public, ignorant of it all, were going to applaud the crimi-
nal, this Dora Nani, and would they care even
if they knew that the heartbroken mother
was weeping bitter tears on her account?

Her son, her only son, how she had loved
him, and how anxious she had been; he was
so delicate, so impressionable, and so prone to
look on the bright side of everything.

Widowed early, she had often deprived herself of the necessities of life in order to assure
him an education, and while she feared the
trend of his adventurous spirit, she was proud
of his rapid progress, of the admiration called
forth by his good looks, and of the general
recognition of his intelligence. Then came the
departure for Paris.

With what supplicating words and gestures
had she given him her blessing at the moment

of leavetaking, and alas! how soon had he been led astray!

Instead of devoting his time to serious studies, he had given himself up to the frivolities of literature, had frequented theatres which were to be condemned, had made the acquaintance of creatures of perdition and linked himself with them. To the sad complaints of his mother, he replied with phrases which distressed her; he spoke of the shortness of life and the uncertainty of what followed, of the enthusiasm which beauty provoked, and affirmed that beauty alone deserved to be worshipped.

He was in no sympathy with what was considered the true life. Why give one's self up to austerity and the useless round of duties instead of admiring the light which shone; instead of draining the joys which were offered; instead of intoxicating one's self with pleasures supplied by nature's prodigal hand. So well had he followed out his theories that, enslaved by vice, he had compromised his honor, and, in order to meet the demands of

Dora Nani, had stolen, and had finally sought in death an escape from disgrace. But what sort of a woman could this Dora Nani be to exert such power of fascination over a young man as to make him sacrifice everything, even his morality, his honesty and his life.

Madame Dolland asked herself this question as the picture she had just seen continued to present itself before her eyes. In spite of her affliction it cast a spell over her. It seemed to become alive, to lean toward her and whisper in her ear. Madame Dolland made a gesture as if to ward it off, but behind her lowered lids she saw the picture even more distinct. It was still tempting her; it made signs; it murmured, "You have only to go to the theatre; you will see, know and judge for yourself." A suggestion of the evil one which must be resisted. The temptation, however, became more powerful, and the resistance of Madame Dolland weaker, and the conflict lasted during the whole almost endless day.

That evening the widow who had thought it necessary to make some improvements in her toilet, some old lace added at the neck and wrists, appeared with the crowd at the ticket window. The price of a seat seemed exorbitant, and she paid it with a twinge of conscience that the money had not gone into the poor box, but, promising herself to go to confession in the morning, she turned with hesitation toward the interior of the theatre.

The splendor of the place impressed her; everything was new to her. On principle as much as from necessity, Madame Dolland had never entered a theatre. She saluted ceremoniously the woman who showed her to the seat, and apologized for disturbing her neighbors. Shyly she studied the boxes, the crystal chandeliers and the mystery of the lowered curtain. The music fascinated her, but at the same time irritated her nerves. Although her heart beat rapidly, she did not experience the sensation of grief which she had dreaded, but rather a sort of feverish curiosity for which she reproached herself. "My son, my son, what would he say?" she thought, and furtively, in order to conciliate heaven, she began to tell her beads.

The three raps sounded, the curtain rose, and at the same time a gust of cold air rushed out into the auditorium. Madame Dolland shivered.

A scene of fairyland was revealed. A lake tinted by the rays of the setting sun with the colonnade of a marble palace extended along its border. On the steps appeared the princess; the applause was deafening. Awaiting silence, Dora Nani remained in an attitude of modesty as if a stranger to the ovation of which she was the recipient. To all appearance she was lost in a trance, and there was a far-away look in her eyes as she gazed into space. Her beautiful bare arms emerged from her dress of pure white, and her whole figure was lighted up by the flickering rays of the dying sunlight. Madame Dolland had never imagined anything to equal it. The scene appeared to her more beautiful than the church decorated for Easter-tide. Dora Nani in her halo of blonde tresses, in her garb of innocence, which the blood-red sun seemed to smirch, was a saintly picture calculated to bring tears to the eyes.

Madame Dolland was annoyed at the comparison and endeavored to resist the fascination which had taken possession of her.

Then Dora Nani began to speak. The tone of her voice was low and serious; it caressed; it moved; it enchanted. Madame Dolland was subjugated.

The actress advanced. The grace of her movements made her appear more beautiful than in repose. Madame Dolland did not take her eyes away from her. She paid scant attention to the coming and going of the other personages or to the dialogue. All her interest in the piece was concentrated upon Dora Nani and she *admired* her. At the fall of the curtain, Madame Dolland applauded. During the *entr' acte* she did not stir from her place. She was as if in a dream, and experienced an indescribable sensation of combined joy and bitterness. She seemed to be learning only now what life really meant.

"Her son had known Dora Nani," and she was conscious of a feeling of pride mingled with grief.

During the following acts, and in proportion as the plot was unfolded, she was taken more and more by the artiste. She saw her with the eyes of her son; she thought she heard him say "Beauty alone merits our worship," and, shaken in all her beliefs of yesterday, she approved of the sentiment. So when Dora Nani at the end of the play marvelously expired in the presence of the audience, Madame Dolland sobbed:

"How she must have suffered."

She thought: "No doubt when she expires like this she recalls him who loved her enough to die for her beauty, and she probably makes it a sort of self-inflicted chastisement to pass through these frequent pangs of agony."

❖

In her simple soul Madame Dolland believed this, and one cannot be blamed for smiling. Madame Dolland, however, was ignorant that life is a comedy and that tragedy only appears as a seasoning.

The emotions of the evening were too strong to allow the poor woman to sleep. She did not even lie down, but in the narrowness of her bedchamber sought to reconcile her present impressions with her former scruples.

She undertook to write to Dora Nani, but what to say and what not to say! She made copies of letters which she filled with erasures; her thoughts were contradictory. Dora Nani so lovely—her son—the worship of beauty—religion—duty——

Madame Dolland lost herself in a world of reflections in proportion as her sensations grew less. At daybreak she became calm, and writing on her visiting card these words, "A mother who forgives you," she put it in an envelope, addressed it, and, going out, dropped it into the nearest letter box.

Then, as on the previous day, she directed her steps toward the church, but on passing the poster did not even glance at it. She knelt before the altar and prayed fervently for herself, her son, and for Dora Nani.

A PARTIAL LIST OF SNUGGLY BOOKS

Printed in the USA
CPSIA information can be obtained
at www.ICGtesting.com
LVHW040354220124
769411LV00104B/1109